MY FATHER'S DRAGON

MY FATHER'S DRAGON

by Ruth Stiles Gannett

Illustrated by Ruth Chrisman Gannett

KODANSHA

Published by Kodansha Ltd., 12–21 Otowa2-chome, Bunkyo-ku, Tokyo 112–8001.

MY FATHER'S DRAGON written by Ruth Stiles Gannett, illustrated by Ruth Chrisman Gannett.
Text Copyright © 1948 by Ruth Stiles Gannett.
Illustrations Copyright © 1948 by Ruth Chrisman Gannett.

English language reprint in a paperback edition with Japanese annotations rights by arrangement with Random House Children's Books, a division of Random House, Inc., through Tuttle-Mori Agency, Inc., Tokyo.
All rights reserved. Printed in Japan.

ISBN 978-4-7700-2636-1

CONTENTS

A Note from the Author 7

1. My Father Meets the Cat 13
2. My Father Runs Away 19
3. My Father Finds the Island 27
4. My Father Finds the River 37
5. My Father Meets Some Tigers 45
6. My Father Meets a Rhinoceros 55
7. My Father Meets a Lion 65
8. My Father Meets a Gorilla 73
9. My Father Makes a Bridge 83
10. My Father Finds the Dragon 90

Notes 102

A Note from the Author

When I wrote it, I had no idea that my story about Elmer and his dragon would become such a success. *My Father's Dragon* was written to amuse myself while between jobs. I wrote it for fun, with no expectation of publication. What a happy surprise it was when Random House accepted it!

Turning my story into a book was a family project. My stepmother was chosen to do the illustrations, and my husband-to-be chose the type. It was a happy collaboration. And when the book appeared in 1948, it promptly won an award—it became a Newbery Honor Book.

The second and third stories, *Elmer and the Dragon* and *The Dragons of Blueland*, came along a few years later. These stories were harder to write than the first one. *My Father's Dragon* had seemed to write itself and I wasn't sure if I could write a sequel, but I did, twice. Since then, my dragon stories have been translated into eight languages and have been read by children all over the world.

Through the years, readers have asked for a fourth story, even offering plots to consider. I have thanked them but declined, while encouraging them to write their own. For myself, I prefer to leave Elmer and Boris and his family safe at home.

Ruth Stiles Gannett

MY FATHER'S DRAGON

Chapter
One

✿

MY FATHER MEETS THE CAT

One cold rainy day when my father was a little boy, he met an old alley cat on his street. The cat was very drippy and uncomfortable so my father said, "Wouldn't you like to come home with me?"

This surprised the cat—she had never before met anyone who cared about old alley cats—but she said, "I'd be very much obliged if I could sit by a warm furnace, and perhaps have a saucer of milk."

"We have a very nice furnace to sit by," said my father, "and I'm sure my mother has an extra saucer of milk."

My father and the cat became good friends but my father's mother was very upset about the cat. She hated cats, particularly ugly old alley cats. "Elmer Elevator," she said to my father, "if you think I'm going to give that cat a saucer of milk, you're very wrong. Once you start feeding stray alley cats you might as well expect to feed every stray in town, and I am *not* going to do it!"

This made my father very sad, and he apologized to the cat because his mother had been so rude. He told the cat to stay anyway, and that somehow he would bring her a saucer of milk each day. My father fed the cat for three weeks, but one day his mother found the cat's saucer in the cellar and she was extremely angry. She whipped my father and threw the cat out the door, but later on my father sneaked out and found the cat. Together they went for a walk in the park and tried to think of nice things

to talk about. My father said, "When I grow up I'm going to have an airplane. Wouldn't it be wonderful to fly just anywhere you might think of!"

"Would you like to fly very, very much?" asked the cat.

"I certainly would. I'd do anything if I could fly."

"Well," said the cat, "if you'd really like to fly that much, I think I know of a sort of a way you might get to fly while you're still a little boy."

"You mean you know where I could get an airplane?"

"Well, not exactly an airplane, but something even better. As you can see, I'm an old cat now, but in my younger days I was quite a traveler. My traveling days are over but last spring I took just one more trip and sailed to the Island of Tangerina, stopping at the port of Cranberry. Well, it just so happened that I missed the boat, and while waiting for the next I thought I'd look around a bit. I was particularly interested in a place called Wild Island, which we had passed on our way to Tangerina. Wild Island and Tangerina are joined together by a long string of rocks, but people never go to Wild Island because it's mostly jungle and inhabited by very wild animals. So I decided to go across the rocks and explore it for myself. It certainly is an interesting place, but I saw something there that made me want to weep."

Chapter
Two

✿

MY FATHER RUNS AWAY

"Wild Island is practically cut in two by a very wide and muddy river," continued the cat. "This river begins near one end of the island and flows into the ocean at the other. Now the animals there

are very lazy, and they used to hate having to go all the way around the beginning of this river to get to the other side of the island. It made visiting inconvenient and mail deliveries slow, particularly during the Christmas rush. Crocodiles could have carried passengers and mail across the river, but crocodiles are very moody, and not the least bit dependable, and are always looking for something to eat. They don't care if the animals have to walk around the river, so that's just what the animals did for many years."

"But what does all this have to do with airplanes?" asked my father, who thought the cat was taking an awfully long time to explain.

"Be patient, Elmer," said the cat, and she went on with the story. "One day about four months before I arrived on Wild Island a baby dragon fell from a low-flying cloud onto the bank of the river. He was too

young to fly very well, and besides, he had bruised one wing quite badly, so he couldn't get back to his cloud. The animals found him soon afterwards and everybody said, 'Why, this is just exactly what we've needed all these years!' They tied a big rope around his neck and waited for the wing to get well. This was going to end all their crossing-the-river troubles."

"I've never seen a dragon," said my father. "Did you see him? How big is he?"

"Oh, yes, indeed I saw the dragon. In fact, we became great friends," said the cat. "I used to hide in the bushes and talk to him when nobody was around. He's not a very big dragon, about the size of a large black bear, although I imagine he's grown quite a bit since I left. He's got a long tail and yellow and blue stripes. His horn and eyes and the bottoms of his feet are bright red, and he has gold-colored wings."

"Oh, how wonderful!" said my father. "What did the animals do with him when his wing got well?"

"They started training him to carry passengers, and even though he is just a baby dragon, they work him all day and all night too sometimes. They make him carry loads that are much too heavy, and if he complains, they twist his wings and beat him.

He's always tied to a stake on a rope just long enough to go across the river. His only friends are the crocodiles, who say 'Hello' to him once a week if they don't forget. Really, he's the most miserable animal I've ever come across. When I left I promised I'd try to help him someday, although I couldn't see how. The rope around his neck is about the biggest, toughest rope you can imagine, with so many knots it would take days to untie them all.

"Anyway, when you were talking about airplanes, you gave me a good idea. Now, I'm quite sure that if you were able to rescue the dragon, which wouldn't be the least bit easy, he'd let you ride him most anywhere, provided you were nice to him, of course. How about trying it?"

"Oh, I'd love to," said my father, and he was so angry at his mother for being rude to the cat that he didn't feel the least bit sad about running away from home for a while.

That very afternoon my father and the cat went down to the docks to see about ships going to the Island of Tangerina. They found out that a ship would be sailing the next week, so right away they started planning for the rescue of the dragon. The cat was a great help in suggesting things for my father to take with him, and she told him everything she knew about Wild Island. Of course, she was too old to go along.

Everything had to be kept very secret, so when they found or bought anything to take on the trip they hid it behind a rock in the park. The night before my father sailed he borrowed his father's knapsack and he and the cat packed everything very carefully. He took chewing gum, two dozen pink lollipops, a package of rubber bands, black rubber boots, a compass, a toothbrush and a tube of tooth paste, six magnifying glasses, a very sharp jackknife, a comb and a hairbrush, seven hair ribbons of different colors, an empty grain bag with a label saying "Cranberry," some clean clothes, and enough food to last my father while he was on the ship. He couldn't live on mice, so he

took twenty-five peanut butter and jelly sandwiches and six apples, because that's all the apples he could find in the pantry.

When everything was packed my father and the cat went down to the docks to the ship. A night watchman was on duty, so while the cat made loud queer noises to distract his attention, my father ran over the gangplank onto the ship. He went down into the hold and hid among some bags of wheat. The ship sailed early the next morning.

Chapter
Three

✤

MY FATHER FINDS THE ISLAND

My father hid in the hold for six days and nights. Twice he was nearly caught when the ship stopped to take on more cargo. But at last he heard a sailor say that the next port would be Cranberry and that they'd be unloading the wheat there. My father knew that the sailors would send him home if they caught him, so he looked in his knapsack and took out a rubber band and the empty grain bag with the label saying "Cranberry." At the last moment my father got inside the bag, knapsack and all, folded the top of the bag inside, and put the

rubber band around the top. He didn't look just exactly like the other bags but it was the best he could do.

Soon the sailors came to unload. They lowered a big net into the hold and began moving the bags of wheat. Suddenly one sailor yelled, "Great Scott! This is the queerest bag of wheat I've ever seen! It's all lumpy-like, but the label says it's to go to Cranberry."

The other sailors looked at the bag too, and my father, who was in the bag, of course, tried even harder to look like a bag of wheat. Then another sailor felt the bag and he just happened to get hold of my father's elbow. "I know what this is," he said. "This is a bag of dried corn on the cob," and he dumped my father into the big net along with the bags of wheat.

This all happened in the late afternoon, so late that the merchant in Cranberry who had ordered the wheat didn't count his bags until the next morning. (He was a very punctual man, and never late for dinner.) The sailors told the captain, and the captain wrote down on a piece of paper, that they had delivered one hundred and sixty bags of wheat and one bag of dried corn on the cob. They left the piece of paper for the merchant and sailed away that evening.

My father heard later that the merchant spent the whole next day counting and recounting the bags and feeling each one trying to find the bag of dried corn on the cob. He never found it because as soon as it was dark my father climbed out of the bag, folded it up and put it back in his knapsack. He walked along the shore to a nice sandy place and lay down to sleep.

My father was very hungry when he woke up the next morning. Just as he was looking to see if he had anything left to eat, some-

thing hit him on the head. It was a tangerine. He had been sleeping right under a tree full of big, fat tangerines. And then he remembered that this was the Island of Tangerina. Tangerine trees grew wild everywhere. My father picked as many as he had room for, which was thirty-one, and started off to find Wild Island.

He walked and walked and walked along the shore, looking for the rocks that joined the two islands. He walked all day, and once when he met a fisherman and asked him about Wild Island, the fisherman began to shake and couldn't talk for a long while. It scared him that much, just thinking about it. Finally he said, "Many people have tried to explore Wild Island, but not one has come back alive. We think they were eaten by the wild animals." This didn't bother my father. He kept walking and slept on the beach again that night.

It was beautifully clear the next day, and way down the shore my father could see a long line of rocks leading out into the ocean, and way, way out at the end he could just see a tiny patch of green. He quickly ate seven tangerines and started down the beach.

It was almost dark when he came to the rocks, but there, way out in the ocean, was the patch of green. He sat down and rested a while, remembering that the cat had said, "If you can, go out to the island at night, because then the wild animals won't see you coming along the rocks and you can hide when you get there." So my father picked seven more tangerines, put on his black rubber boots, and waited for dark.

It was a very black night and my father could hardly see the rocks ahead of him. Sometimes they were quite high and sometimes the waves almost covered them, and they were slippery and hard to walk on. Sometimes the rocks were far apart and my father had to get a running start and leap from one to the next.

After a while he began to hear a rumbling noise. It grew louder and louder as he got nearer to the island. At last it seemed as if he was right on top of the noise, and he was. He had jumped from a rock onto the back of a small whale who was fast asleep and cuddled up between two rocks. The whale was snoring and making more noise than a steam shovel, so it never heard my father say, "Oh, I didn't know that was you!" And it never knew my father had jumped on its back by mistake.

For seven hours my father climbed and

slipped and leapt from rock to rock, but while it was still dark he finally reached the very last rock and stepped off onto Wild Island.

Chapter
Four

✿

MY FATHER FINDS THE RIVER

The jungle began just beyond a narrow strip of beach; thick, dark, damp, scary jungle. My father hardly knew where to go, so he crawled under a wahoo bush to think, and ate eight tangerines. The first thing to do, he decided, was to find the river, because the dragon was tied somewhere along its bank. Then he thought, "If the river flows into the ocean, I ought to be able to find it quite easily if I just walk along the beach far enough." So my father walked until the sun rose and he was quite far from the Ocean Rocks. It was dangerous to stay near them because they might be guarded in the daytime. He found a clump of tall grass and sat down. Then he took off his rubber boots and ate three more tangerines. He could have eaten twelve but he hadn't seen any tangerines on this island and he could not risk running out of something to eat.

My father slept all that day and only woke up late in the afternoon when he heard a funny little voice saying, "Queer, queer, what a dear little dock! I mean, dear, dear, what a queer little rock!" My father saw a tiny paw rubbing itself on his knapsack. He lay very still and the mouse, for it *was* a mouse, hurried away muttering to itself, "I must smell tumduddy. I mean, I must tell somebody."

My father waited a few minutes and then started down the beach because it was almost dark now, and he was afraid the mouse really would tell somebody. He walked all night and two scary things happened. First, he just had to sneeze, so he did, and somebody close by said, "Is that you, Monkey?" My father said, "Yes." Then the voice said, "You must have something on your back, Monkey," and my father said "Yes," because he did. He had his knapsack on his back. "What do you have on your back, Monkey?" asked the voice.

My father didn't know what to say because what would a monkey have on its back, and how would it sound telling someone about it if it did have something? Just then another voice said, "I bet you're taking your sick grandmother to the doctor's." My

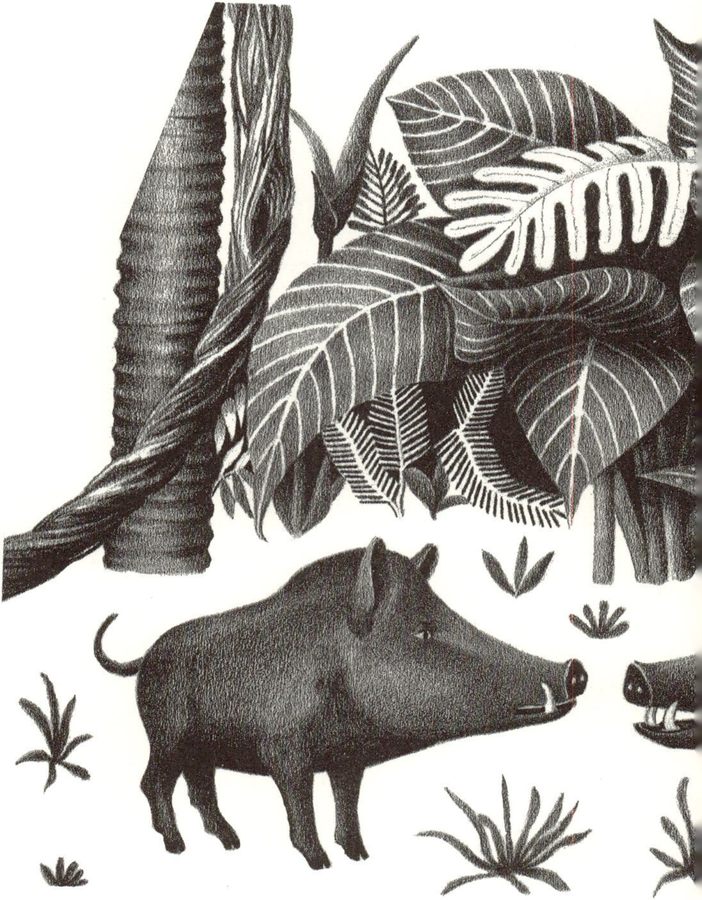

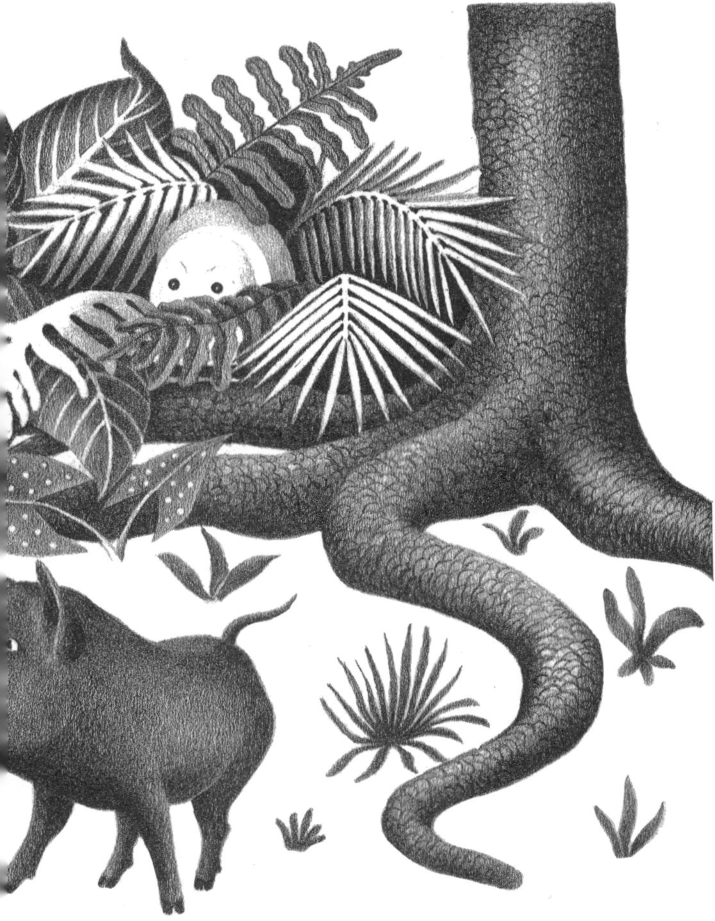

father said "Yes" and hurried on. Quite by accident he found out later that he had been talking to a pair of tortoises.

The second thing that happened was that he nearly walked right between two wild boars who were talking in low solemn whispers. When he first saw the dark shapes he thought they were boulders. Just in time he heard one of them say, "There are three signs of a recent invasion. First, fresh tangerine peels were found under the wahoo bush near the Ocean Rocks. Second, a mouse reported an extraordinary rock some distance from the Ocean Rocks which upon further investigation simply wasn't there. However, more fresh tangerine peels were found in the same spot, which is the third sign of invasion. Since tangerines do not grow on our island, somebody must have brought them across the Ocean Rocks from the other island, which may, or may not, have something to do with the appearance and/or disappearance of the extraordinary rock reported by the mouse."

After a long silence the other boar said, "You know, I think we're taking all this too seriously. Those peels probably floated over here all by themselves, and you know how unreliable mice are. Besides, if there had been an invasion, *I* would have seen it!"

"Perhaps you're right," said the first boar. "Shall we retire?" Whereupon they both trundled back into the jungle.

Well, that taught my father a lesson, and after that he saved all his tangerine peels. He walked all night and toward morning came to the river. Then his troubles really began.

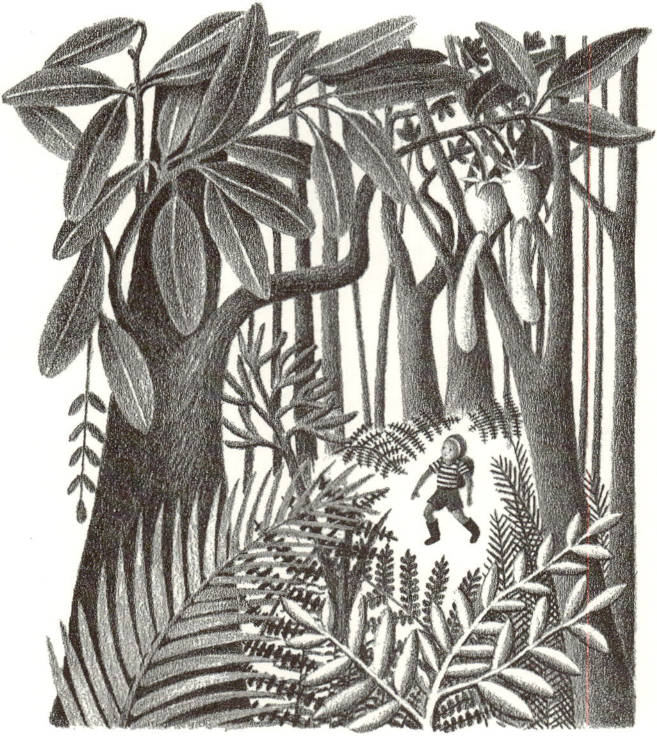

Chapter
Five

❀

MY FATHER MEETS SOME TIGERS

The river was very wide and muddy, and the jungle was very gloomy and dense. The trees grew close to each other, and what room there was between them was taken up by great high ferns with sticky leaves. My father hated to leave the beach, but he decided to start along the river bank where at least the jungle wasn't quite so thick. He ate three tangerines, making sure to keep all the peels this time, and put on his rubber boots.

My father tried to follow the river bank but it was very swampy, and as he went farther the swamp became deeper. When it was almost as deep as his boot tops he got stuck in the oozy, mucky mud. My father tugged and tugged, and nearly pulled his boots right off, but at last he managed to wade to a drier place. Here the jungle was so thick that he could hardly see where the river was. He unpacked his compass and figured out the direction he should walk in order to stay near the river. But he didn't know that the river made a very sharp curve away from him just a little way beyond, and so as he walked straight ahead he was getting farther and farther away from the river.

It was very hard to walk in the jungle. The sticky leaves of the ferns caught at my father's hair, and he kept tripping over roots and rotten logs. Sometimes the trees were clumped so closely together that he couldn't squeeze between them and had to walk a long way around.

He began to hear whispery noises, but he couldn't see any animals anywhere. The deeper into the jungle he went the surer he was that something was following him, and then he thought he heard whispery noises on both sides of him as well as behind. He tried to run, but he tripped over more roots, and the noises only came nearer. Once or twice he thought he heard something laughing at him.

At last he came out into a clearing and ran right into the middle of it so that he could see anything that might try to attack him. Was he surprised when he looked and saw fourteen green eyes coming out of the jungle all around the clearing, and when the green eyes turned into seven tigers! The tigers walked around him in a big circle, looking hungrier all the time, and then they sat down and began to talk.

"I suppose you thought we didn't know you were trespassing in our jungle!"

Then the next tiger spoke. "I suppose you're going to say you didn't know it was our jungle!"

"Did you know that not one explorer has ever left this island alive?" said the third tiger.

My father thought of the cat and knew this wasn't true. But of course he had too much sense to say so. One doesn't contradict a hungry tiger.

The tigers went on talking in turn. "You're our first little boy, you know. I'm curious to know if you're especially tender."

"Maybe you think we have regular mealtimes, but we don't. We just eat whenever we're feeling hungry," said the fifth tiger.

"And we're very hungry right now. In fact, I can hardly wait," said the sixth.

"I *can't* wait!" said the seventh tiger.

And then all the tigers said together in a loud roar, "Let's begin right now!" and they moved in closer.

My father looked at those seven hungry tigers, and then he had an idea. He quickly opened his knapsack and took out the chewing gum. The cat had told him that tigers were especially fond of chewing gum, which was very scarce on the island. So he threw them each a piece but they only growled, "As fond as we are of chewing gum, we're sure we'd like you even better!" and they moved so close that he could feel them breathing on his face.

"But this is very special chewing gum," said my father. "If you keep on chewing it long enough it will turn green, and then if you plant it, it will grow more chewing gum, and the sooner you start chewing the sooner you'll have more."

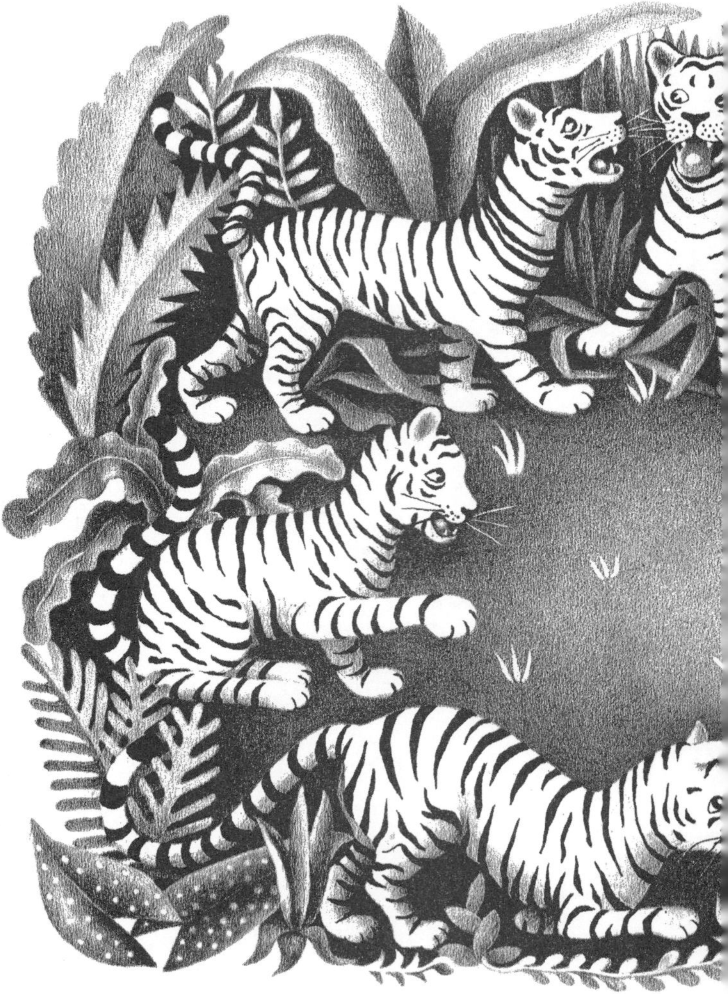

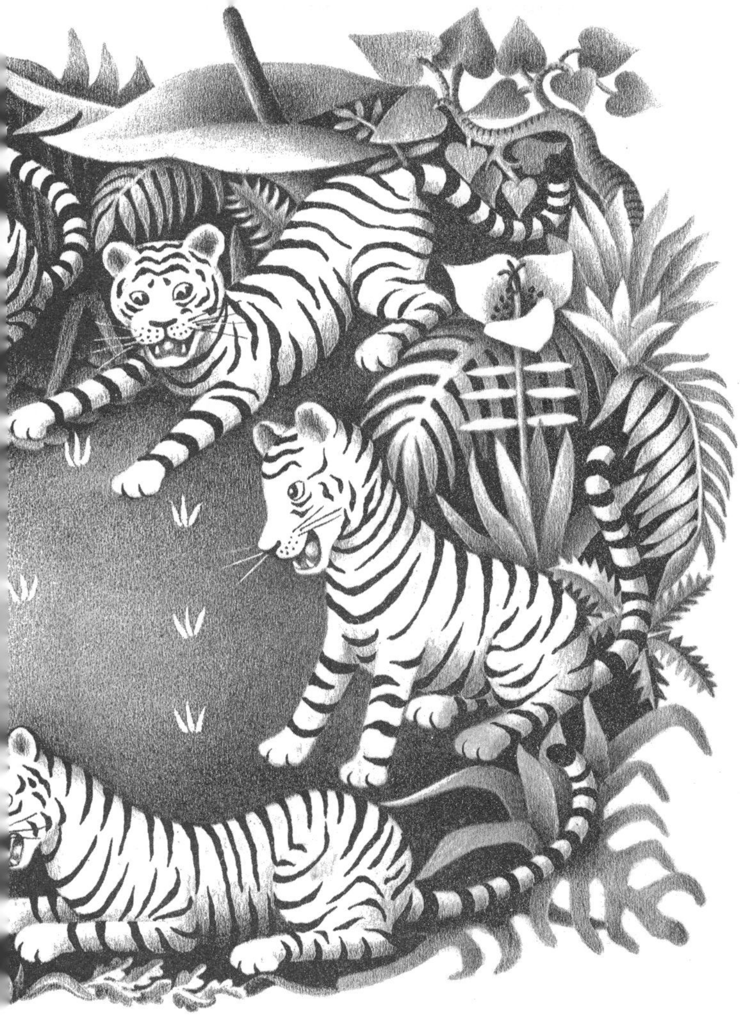

The tigers said, "Why, you don't say! Isn't that fine!" And as each one wanted to be the first to plant the chewing gum, they all unwrapped their pieces and began chewing as hard as they could. Every once in a while one tiger would look into another's mouth and say, "Nope, it's not done yet," until finally they were all so busy looking into each other's mouths to make sure that no one was getting ahead that they forgot all about my father.

Chapter
Six

✿

MY FATHER MEETS A RHINOCEROS

My father soon found a trail leading away from the clearing. All sorts of animals might be using it too, but he decided to follow the trail no matter what he met because it might lead to the dragon. He kept a sharp lookout in front and behind and went on.

Just as he was feeling quite safe, he came around a curve right behind the two wild boars. One of them was saying to the other, "Did you know that the tortoises thought they saw Monkey carrying his sick grandmother to the doctor's last night? But Monkey's grandmother died a week ago, so they must have seen something else. I wonder what it was."

"I told you that there was an invasion afoot," said the other boar, "and I intend to find out what it is. I simply can't stand invasions."

"Nee meither," said a tiny little voice. "I mean, me neither," and my father knew that the mouse was there, too.

"Well," said the first boar, "you search the trail up this way to the dragon. I'll go back down the other way through the big clearing, and we'll send Mouse to watch the Ocean Rocks in case the invasion should decide to go away before we find it."

My father hid behind a mahogany tree just in time, and the first boar walked right past him. My father waited for the other boar to get a head start on him, but he didn't wait very long because he knew that when the first boar saw the tigers chewing gum in the clearing, he'd be even more suspicious.

Soon the trail crossed a little brook and my father, who by this time was very thirsty, stopped to get a drink of water. He still had on his rubber boots, so he waded into a little pool of water and was stooping down when something quite sharp picked him up by the seat of the pants and shook him very hard.

"Don't you know that's my private weeping pool?" said a deep angry voice.

My father couldn't see who was talking

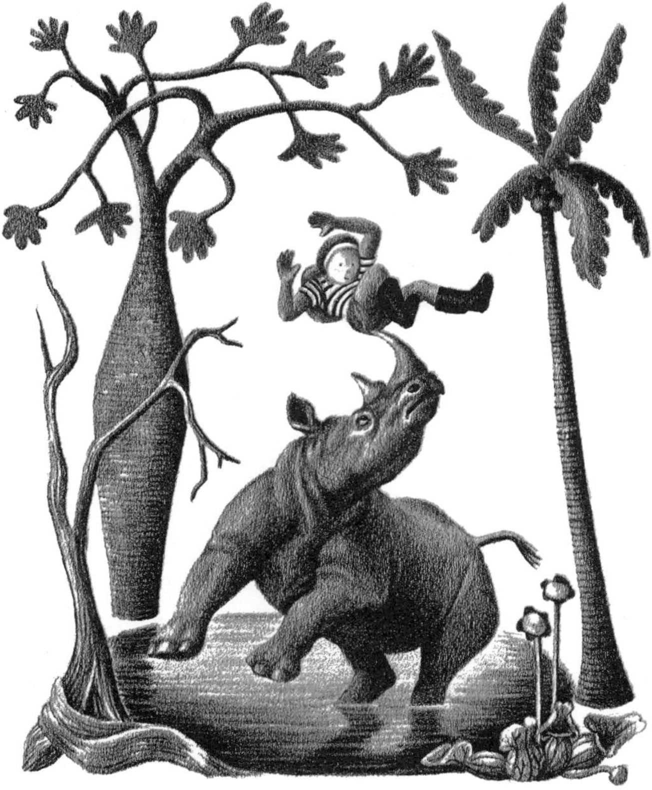

because he was hanging in the air right over the pool, but he said, "Oh, no, I'm so sorry. I didn't know that everybody had a private weeping pool."

"Everybody doesn't!" said the angry voice, "but I do because I have such a big thing to weep about, and I drown everybody I find using my weeping pool." With that the animal tossed my father up and down over the water.

"What—is it—that—you—weep about—so much?" asked my father, trying to get his breath, and he thought over all the things he had in his pack.

"Oh, I have many things to weep about, but the biggest thing is the color of my tusk." My father squirmed every which way trying to see the tusk, but it was through the seat of his pants where he couldn't possibly see it. "When I was a young rhinoceros, my tusk was pearly white," said the animal (and then my father knew that he was hanging by the seat of his pants from a rhinoceros' tusk!), "but it has turned a nasty yellow-gray in my old age, and I find it very ugly. You see, everything else about me is ugly, but when I had a beautiful tusk I didn't worry so much about the rest. Now that my tusk is ugly too, I can't sleep nights just thinking about how completely ugly I am, and I weep all the time. But why should I be telling you these things? I caught you using my pool and now I'm going to drown you."

"Oh, wait a minute, Rhinoceros," said my father. "I have some things that will make your tusk all white and beautiful again. Just let me down and I'll give them to you."

The rhinoceros said, "You do? I can hardly believe it! Why, I'm so excited!" He put my father down and danced around in a circle while my father got out the tube of tooth paste and the toothbrush.

"Now," said my father, "just move your tusk a little nearer, please, and I'll show you how to begin." My father wet the brush in the pool, squeezed on a dab of tooth paste, and scrubbed very hard in one tiny spot. Then he told the rhinoceros to wash it off, and when the pool was calm again, he told the rhinoceros to look in the water and see how white the little spot was. It was hard to see in the dim light of the jungle, but sure enough, the spot shone pearly white, just like new. The rhinoceros was so pleased that he grabbed the toothbrush and began scrubbing violently, forgetting all about my father.

Just then my father heard hoof steps and he jumped behind the rhinoceros. It was the boar coming back from the big clearing where the tigers were chewing gum. The boar looked at the rhinoceros, and at the toothbrush, and at the tube of tooth paste,

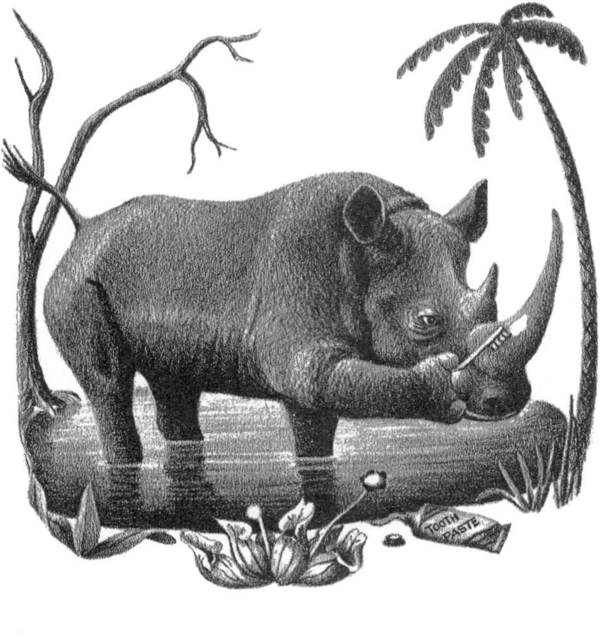
TOOTH PASTE

and then he scratched his ear on a tree. "Tell me, Rhinoceros," he said, "where did you get that fine tube of tooth paste and that toothbrush?"

"Too busy!" said the rhinoceros, and he went on brushing as hard as he could.

The boar sniffed angrily and trotted down the trail toward the dragon, muttering to himself, "Very suspicious—tigers too busy chewing gum, Rhinoceros too busy brushing his tusk—must get hold of that invasion. Don't like it one bit, not one bit! It's upsetting everybody terribly—wonder what it's doing here, anyway."

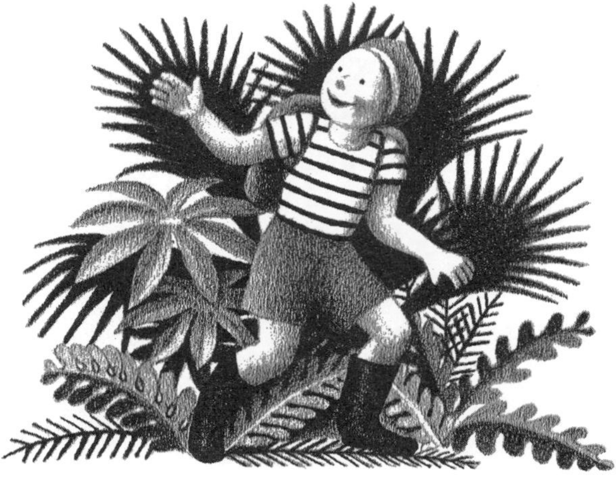

Chapter
Seven

✿

MY FATHER MEETS A LION

My father waved goodbye to the rhinoceros, who was much too busy to notice, got a drink farther down the brook, and waded back to the trail. He hadn't gone very far when he heard an angry animal roaring, "Ding blast it! I told you not to go blackberrying yesterday. Won't you ever learn? What will your mother say!"

My father crept along and peered into a small clearing just ahead. A lion was prancing about clawing at his mane, which was all snarled and full of blackberry twigs. The more he clawed the worse it became and the madder he grew and the more he yelled at himself, because it was himself he was yelling at all the time.

My father could see that the trail went through the clearing, so he decided to crawl around the edge in the underbrush and not disturb the lion.

He crawled and crawled, and the yelling grew louder and louder. Just as he was about to reach the trail on the other side the yelling suddenly stopped. My father looked around and saw the lion glaring at him. The lion charged and skidded to a stop a few inches away.

"Who are you?" the lion yelled at my father.

"My name is Elmer Elevator."

"Where do you think you are going?"

"I'm going home," said my father.

"That's what you think!" said the lion. "Ordinarily I'd save you for afternoon tea,

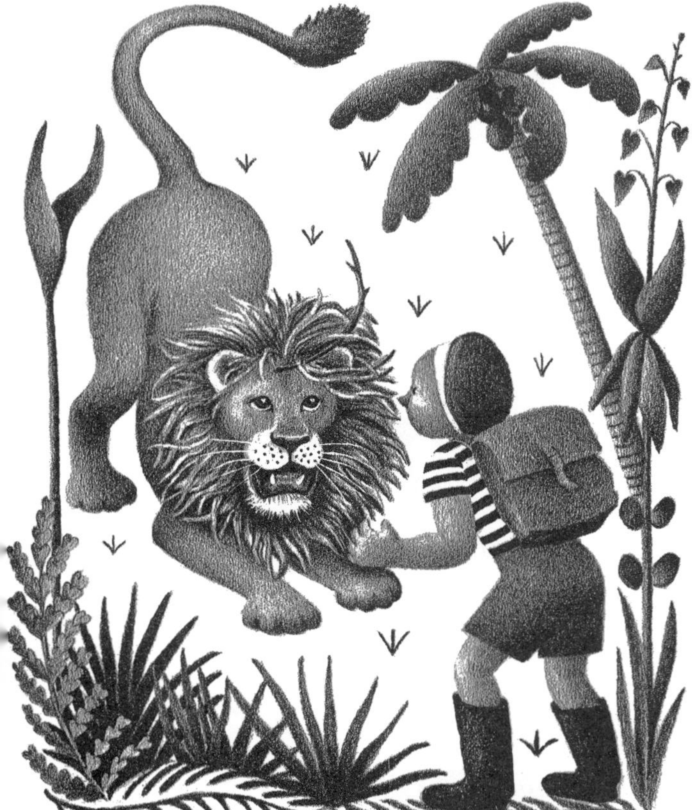

but I happen to be upset enough and hungry enough to eat you right now." And he picked up my father in his front paws to feel how fat he was.

My father said, "Oh, please, Lion, before you eat me, tell me why you are so particularly upset today."

"It's my mane," said the lion, as he was figuring how many bites a little boy would make. "You see what a dreadful mess it is, and I don't seem to be able to do anything about it. My mother is coming over on the dragon this afternoon, and if she sees me this way I'm afraid she'll stop my allowance. She can't stand messy manes! But I'm going to eat you now, so it won't make any difference to you."

"Oh, wait a minute," said my father, "and I'll give you just the things you need to make your mane all tidy and beautiful. I have them here in my pack."

"You do?" said the lion. "Well, give them to me, and perhaps I'll save you for afternoon tea after all," and he put my father down on the ground.

My father opened the pack and took out the comb and the brush and the seven hair ribbons of different colors. "Look," he said, "I'll show you what to do on your forelock, where you can watch me. First you brush a while, and then you comb, and then you brush again until all the twigs and snarls are gone. Then you divide it up in three and braid it like this and tie a ribbon around the end."

As my father was doing this, the lion watched very carefully and began to look much happier. When my father tied on the ribbon he was all smiles. "Oh, that's wonderful, really wonderful!" said the lion. "Let me have the comb and brush and see if I can do it." So my father gave him the comb and

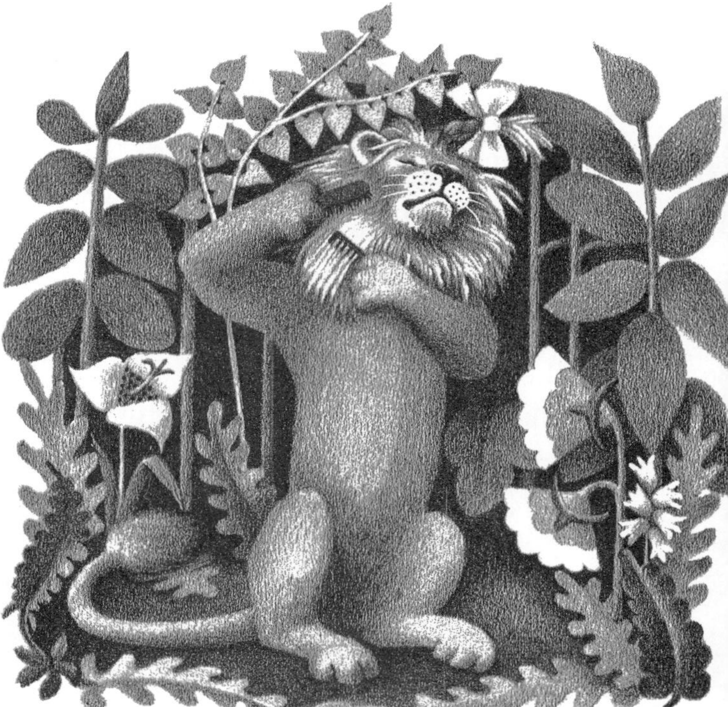

brush and the lion began busily grooming his mane. As a matter of fact, he was so busy that he didn't even know when my father left.

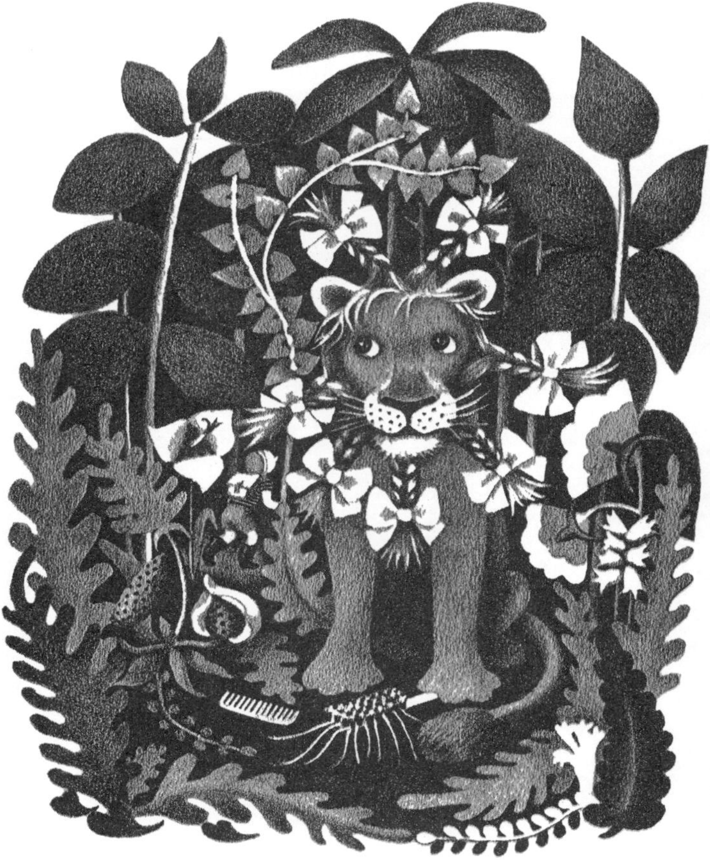

Chapter
Eight

✿

MY FATHER MEETS A GORILLA

My father was very hungry so he sat down under a baby banyan tree on the side of the trail and ate four tangerines. He wanted to eat eight or ten, but he had only thirteen left and it might be a long time before he could get more. He packed away all the peels and was about to get up when he heard the familiar voices of the boars.

"I wouldn't have believed it if I hadn't seen them with my own eyes, but wait and see for yourself. All the tigers are sitting around chewing gum to beat the band. Old Rhinoceros is so busy brushing his tusk that he doesn't even look around to see who's going by, and they're all so busy they won't even talk to me!"

"Horsefeathers!" said the other boar, now very close to my father. "They'll talk to me! I'm going to get to the bottom of this if it's the last thing I do!"

The voices passed my father and went around a curve, and he hurried on because he knew how much more upset the boars would be when they saw the lion's mane tied up in hair ribbons.

Before long my father came to a crossroads and he stopped to read the signs.

Straight ahead an arrow pointed to the Beginning of the River; to the left, the Ocean Rocks; and to the right, to the Dragon Ferry. My father was reading all these signs when he heard pawsteps and ducked behind the signpost. A beautiful lioness paraded past and turned down toward the clearings. Although she could have seen my father if she had bothered to glance at the post, she was much too occupied looking dignified to see anything but the tip of her own nose. It was the lion's mother, of course, and that, thought my father, must mean that the dragon was on this side of the river. He hurried on but it was farther away than he had judged. He finally came to the river bank in the late afternoon and looked all around, but there was no dragon anywhere in sight. He must have gone back to the other side.

My father sat down under the palm tree and was trying to have a good idea when something big and black and hairy jumped out of the tree and landed with a loud crash at his feet.

"Well?" said a huge voice.

"Well what?" said my father, for which he was very sorry when he looked up and discovered he was talking to an enormous and very fierce gorilla.

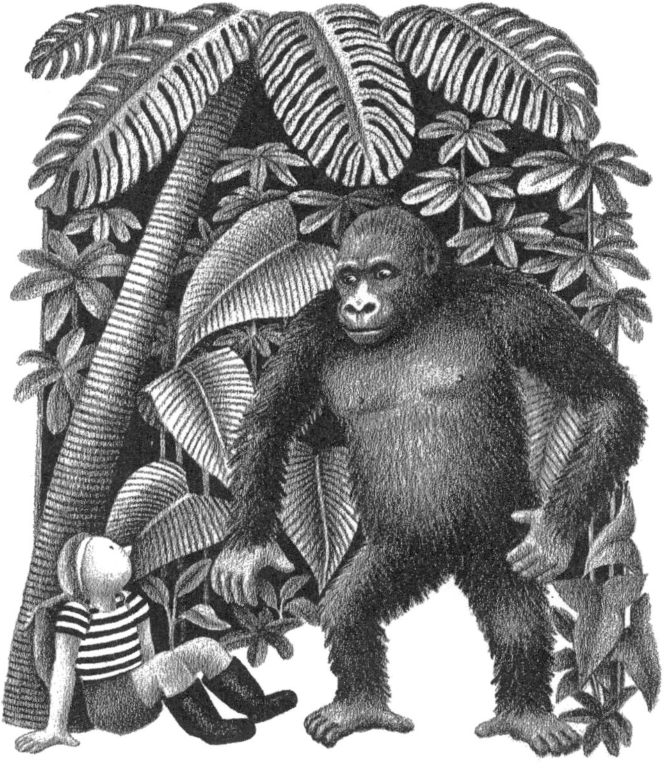

"Well, explain yourself," said the gorilla. "I'll give you till ten to tell me your name, business, your age, and what's in that pack," and he began counting to ten as fast as he could.

My father didn't even have time to say "Elmer Elevator, explorer" before the gorilla interrupted, "Too slow! I'll twist your arms the way I twist that dragon's wings, and then we'll see if you can't hurry up a bit." He grabbed my father's arms, one in each fist, and was just about to twist them when he suddenly let go and began scratching his chest with both hands.

"Blast those fleas!" he raged. "They won't give you a moment's peace, and the worst of it is that you can't even get a good look at them. Rosie! Rhoda! Rachel! Ruthie! Ruby! Roberta! Come here and get rid of this flea on my chest. It's driving me crazy!"

Six little monkeys tumbled out of the

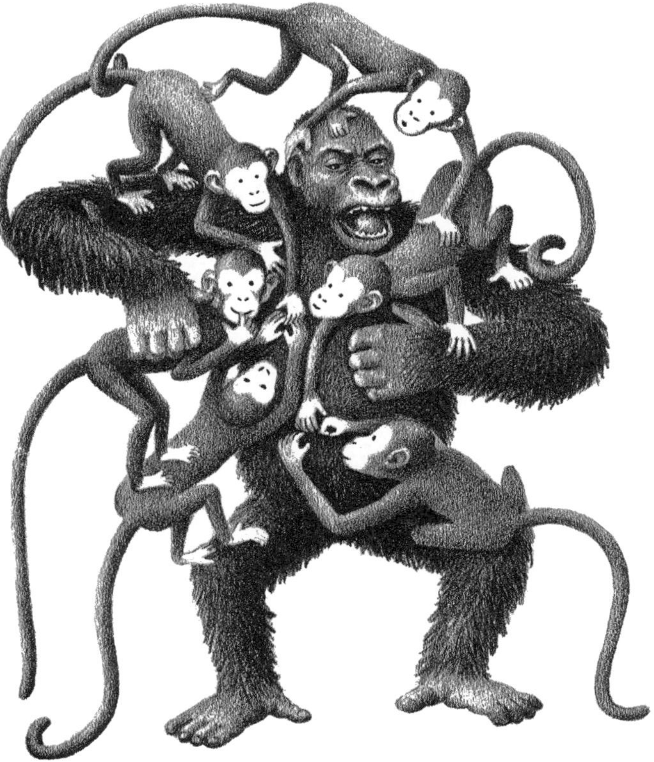

palm tree, dashed to the gorilla, and began combing the hair on his chest.

"Well," said the gorilla, "it's still there!"

"We're looking, we're looking," said the six little monkeys, "but they're awfully hard to see, you know."

"I know," said the gorilla, "but hurry. I've got work to do," and he winked at my father.

"Oh, Gorilla," said my father, "in my knapsack I have six magnifying glasses. They'd be just the thing for hunting fleas."

My father unpacked them and gave one to Rosie, one to Rhoda, one to Rachel, one to Ruthie, one to Ruby, and one to Roberta.

"Why, they're miraculous!" said the six little monkeys. "It's easy to see the fleas now, only there are hundreds of them!" And they went on hunting frantically.

A moment later many more monkeys appeared out of a near-by clump of mangroves and began crowding around to get a look at the fleas through the magnifying glasses. They completely surrounded the gorilla, and he could not see my father nor did he remember to twist his arms.

Chapter
Nine

✿

MY FATHER MAKES A BRIDGE

My father walked back and forth along the bank trying to think of some way to cross the river. He found a high flagpole with a rope going over to the other side. The rope went through a loop at the top of the pole and then down the pole and around a large crank. A sign on the crank said:

TO SUMMON DRAGON, YANK THE CRANK
REPORT DISORDERLY CONDUCT TO GORILLA

From what the cat had told my father, he

knew that the other end of the rope was tied around the dragon's neck, and he felt sorrier than ever for the poor dragon. If he were on this side, the gorilla would twist his wings until it hurt so much that he'd have to fly to the other side. If he were on the other side, the gorilla would crank the rope until the dragon would either choke to death or fly back to this side. What a life for a baby dragon!

My father knew that if he called to the dragon to come across the river, the gorilla would surely hear him, so he thought about climbing the pole and going across the rope. The pole was very high, and even if he could get to the top without being seen he'd have to go all the way across hand over hand. The river was very muddy, and all sorts of unfriendly things might live in it, but my father could think of no other way to get across. He was about to start up the pole when, despite all the noise the monkeys were making, he heard a loud splash behind him. He looked all around in the water but it was dusk now, and he couldn't see anything there.

"It's me, Crocodile," said a voice to the left. "The water's lovely, and I have such a craving for something sweet. Won't you come in for a swim?"

A pale moon came out from behind the clouds and my father could see where the voice was coming from. The crocodile's head was just peeping out of the water.

"Oh, no thank you," said my father. "I never swim after sundown, but I do have something sweet to offer you. Perhaps you'd like a lollipop, and perhaps you have friends who would like lollipops, too?"

"Lollipops!" said the crocodile. "Why, that is a treat! How about it, boys?"

A whole chorus of voices shouted, "Hurrah! Lollipops!" and my father counted as many as seventeen crocodiles with their heads just peeping out of the water.

"That's fine," said my father as he got out the two dozen pink lollipops and the rubber bands. "I'll stick one here in the bank. Lollipops last longer if you keep them out of the

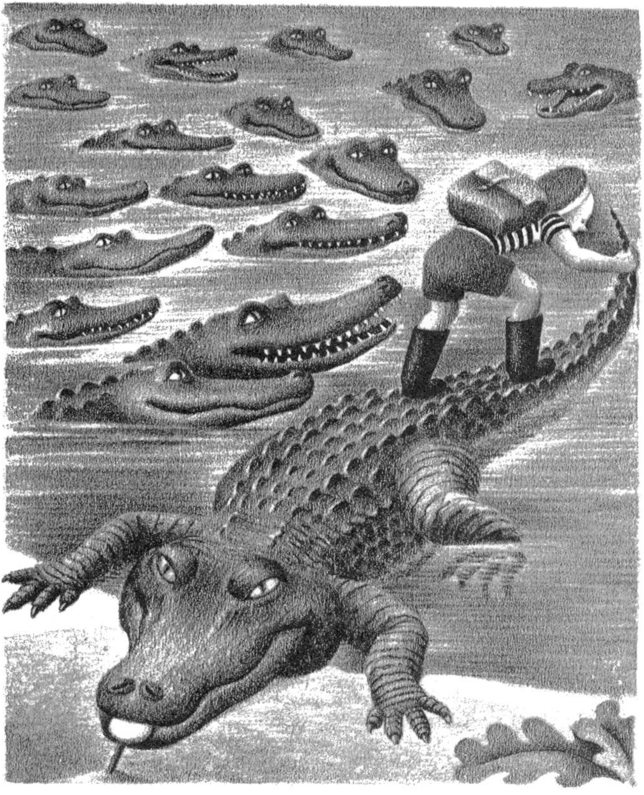

water, you know. Now, one of you can have this one."

The crocodile who had first spoken swam up and tasted it. "Delicious, mighty delicious!" he said.

"Now if you don't mind," said my father, "I'll just walk along your back and fasten another lollipop to the tip of your tail with a rubber band. You don't mind, do you?"

"Oh no, not in the least," said the crocodile.

"Can you get your tail out of the water just a bit?" asked my father.

"Yes, of course," said the crocodile, and he lifted up his tail. Then my father ran along his back and fastened another lollipop with a rubber band.

"Who's next?" said my father, and a second crocodile swam up and began sucking on that lollipop.

"Now, you gentlemen can save a lot of

time if you just line up across the river," said my father, "and I'll be along to give you each a lollipop."

So the crocodiles lined up right across the river with their tails in the air, waiting for my father to fasten on the rest of the lollipops. The tail of the seventeenth crocodile just reached the other bank.

Chapter
Ten

❀

MY FATHER FINDS THE DRAGON

When my father was crossing the back of the fifteenth crocodile with two more lollipops to go, the noise of the monkeys suddenly stopped, and he could hear a much bigger noise getting louder every second. Then he could hear seven furious tigers and one raging rhinoceros and two seething lions and one ranting gorilla along with countless screeching monkeys, led by two extremely irate wild boars, all yelling, "It's a trick! It's a trick! There's an invasion and it must be after our dragon. Kill it! Kill it!"

The whole crowd stampeded down to the bank.

As my father was fixing the seventeenth lollipop for the last crocodile he heard a wild boar scream, "Look, it came this way! It's over there now, see! The crocodiles made a bridge for it," and just as my father leapt onto the other bank one of the wild boars jumped onto the back of the first crocodile. My father didn't have a moment to spare.

By now the dragon realized that my father was coming to rescue him. He ran out of the bushes and jumped up and down yelling, "Here I am! I'm right here! Can you see me? Hurry, the boar is coming over on the crocodiles, too. They're all coming over! Oh, please hurry, hurry!" The noise was simply terrific.

My father ran up to the dragon, and took out his very sharp jackknife. "Steady, old boy, steady. We'll make it. Just stand still," he told the dragon as he began to saw through the big rope.

By this time both boars, all seven tigers, the two lions, the rhinoceros, and the gorilla, along with the countless screeching monkeys, were all on their way across the crocodiles and there was still a lot of rope to cut through.

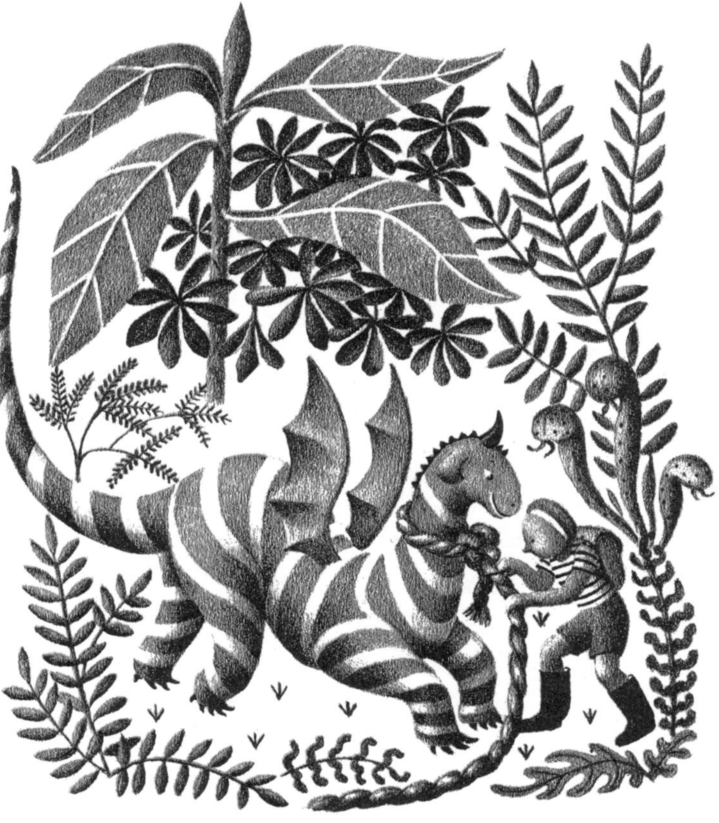

"Oh, hurry," the dragon kept saying, and my father again told him to stand still.

"If I don't think I can make it," said my father, "we'll fly over to the other side of the river and I can finish cutting the rope there."

Suddenly the screaming grew louder and madder and my father thought the animals must have crossed the river. He looked around, and saw something which surprised and delighted him. Partly because he had finished his lollipop, and partly because, as I told you before, crocodiles are very moody and not the least bit dependable and are always looking for something to eat, the first crocodile had turned away from the bank and started swimming down the river. The second crocodile hadn't finished yet, so he followed right after the first, still sucking his lollipop. All the rest did the same thing, one right after the other, until they were all swimming away in a line. The two wild boars, the seven tigers, the rhinoceros, the two lions, the gorilla, along with the countless screeching monkeys, were all riding down the middle of the river on the train of crocodiles sucking pink lollipops, and all yelling and screaming and getting their feet wet.

My father and the dragon laughed themselves weak because it was such a silly sight. As soon as they had recovered, my father finished cutting the rope and the dragon raced around in circles and tried to turn a somersault. He was the most excited baby dragon that ever lived. My father was in a hurry to fly away, and when the dragon finally calmed down a bit my father climbed up onto his back.

"All aboard!" said the dragon. "Where shall we go?"

"We'll spend the night on the beach, and

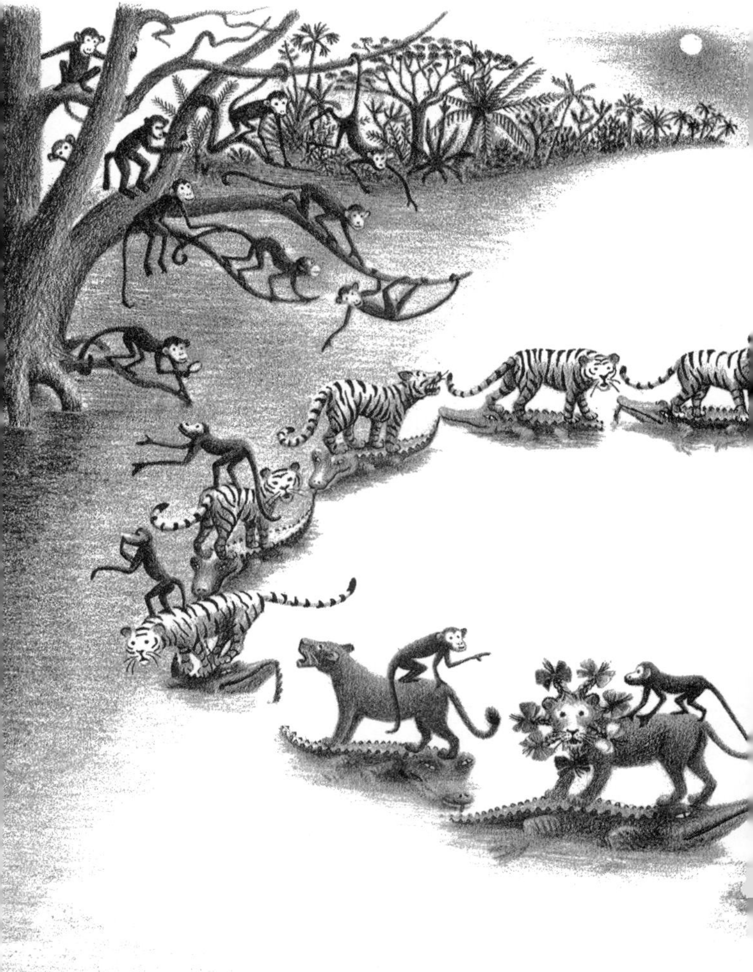

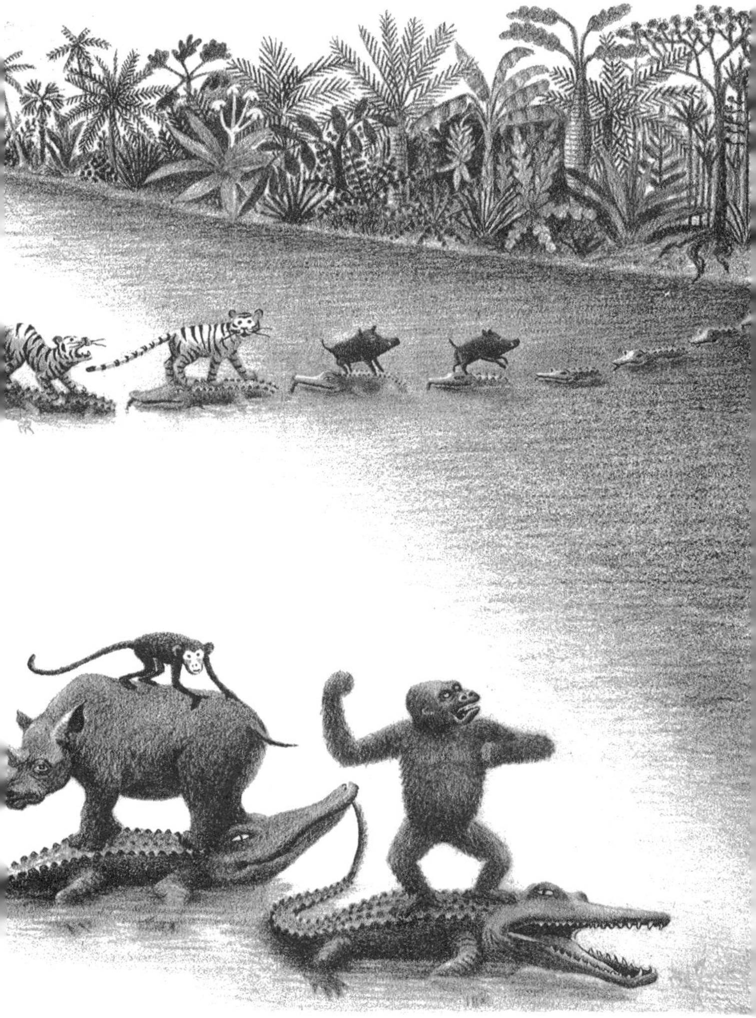

tomorrow we'll start on the long journey home. So, it's off to the shores of Tangerina!" shouted my father as the dragon soared above the dark jungle and the muddy river and all the animals bellowing at them and all the crocodiles licking pink lollipops and grinning wide grins. After all, what did the crocodiles care about a way to cross the river, and what a fine feast they were carrying on their backs!

As my father and the dragon passed over the Ocean Rocks they heard a tiny excited voice scream, "Bum cack! Bum cack! We dreed our nagon! I mean, we need our dragon!"

But my father and the dragon knew that nothing in the world would ever make them go back to Wild Island.

THE END

MAP OF THE ISLAND OF TANGERINA AND WILD ISLAND

CRANBERRY

wild tangerine trees grew all over the island

ISLAND OF TANGERINA

OCEAN RO[CKS]

my father [arrived] here late afternoon waited for

my father slept under this tangerine tree

my father met a fisherman who was too scared even to think about Wild Island

my father slept on this point and saw the rocks the next morning

WILD ISLAND

river begins here

my father doesn't know what's on this side of the island

palmtree and gorilla

sign post

baby Banyan tree

small clearing

flag pole and crank

sleeping whale snoring

Wahoo bushes

dragon in bushes

tangerine peels

brook

clump of tall grass where my father slept and left more tangerine peels

weeping pool

RIVER

my father talked to a pair of tortoises

Mahogany tree

big clearing

swamp

this is all very thick jungle

my father comes to the river and decides to go along the bank

my father nearly walked right between two wild boars

Notes

A Note from the Author 作者前書き

p. 7   **5** to amuse myself 自分の楽しみのために   **8** Random House ランダムハウス(アメリカの出版社)   **10** step-mother まま母   **11** husband-to-be 夫となる人   **12** type 活字   **12** collaboration 共同制作   **14** promptly すぐに   **14** became a Newbery Honor Book ニューベリー賞(アメリカで毎年最も優れた児童文学作品に与えられる)作品となった   **16** *Elmer and the Dragon*「エルマーとりゅう」   **17** *The Dragons of Blueland*「エルマーと16ぴきのりゅう」

p. 8   **4** sequel 続編   **10** plots 筋   **11** declined 辞退した

第1章

My Father Meets the Cat（ぼくのとうさん　ねこにあう）

p. 13   **5** alley cat のらねこ   **6** drippy びしょぬれの   **11** I'd be very much obliged if ... ‥‥したらたいへんありがたいのですが   **12** furnace だんろ   **13** saucer 小皿

p. 15   **7** stray 宿なしの   **12** rude 失礼な   **16** cellar 地下室   **17** whipped むちでたたいた   **19** sneaked out こっそり抜け出した

p. 17   **14** the Island of Tangerina みかん島   **15** the port of Cranberry クランベリー港   **19** Wild Island どうぶつ島   **21** are joined together by a long string of rocks 岩がてんてんとあって、(二つの島が) その岩づたいにつながっていた

p. 18   **2** (is) inhabited by ... ‥‥が住んでいた   **7** weep 泣く

第2章

My Father Runs Away（エルマー　にげだす）

p. 19　4 is practically cut in two by ... 実際には…でまっ二つに分かれている　　5 muddy どろ水の

p. 20　4 inconvenient 不便な　　5 mail deliveries 郵便配達　　8 moody 気まぐれな　　8 not the least bit dependable ぜんぜんあてにならなかった　　13 "But what does all this have to do with airplanes?"「でもその話と飛行機とどういう関係があるの？」

p. 21　1 had bruised one wing quite badly 片方の羽をひどくけがしてしまった　　8 crossing-the-river troubles 川渡りの問題

p. 22　10 horn 角　　19 loads 荷物

p. 23　1 (is) tied to a stake on a rope ロープでくいにつながれていた　　10 knots むすび目　　17 provided you were nice to him りゅうに親切にしてやればですが

p. 24　3 docks 波止場　　18 lollipops 棒つきキャンディ　　19 rubber bands 輪ゴム　　21 magnifying glasses 虫めがね

p. 25　3 grain bag 穀物をいれる袋

p. 26　3 pantry 戸棚　　6 night watchman was on duty 夜まわりの番人が立っていた　　7 made loud queer noises to distract his attention おかしな鳴き声をだして注意をそらした　　9 gangplank 船のタラップ　　10 hold 船倉　　11 wheat 小麦

第3章

My Father Finds the Island（エルマー　しまをみつける）

p. 29　7 Great Scott! こりゃたまげた！　　8 all lumpy-like でこぼこだらけ　　16 dried corn on the cob 芯のついたままの乾燥とうもろこし　　17 dumped 投げ込んだ　　20 merchant 商人

p. 30　**3** punctual 時間を守る

p. 31　**1** tangerine みかん (タンジェリンオレンジ)

p. 33　**12** had to get a running start and leap from one to the next 助走をつけて、次の岩に飛びうつらなければならなかった　**14** rumbling noise ゴロゴロいう音　**19** was fast asleep and cuddled up between two rocks 二つの岩の間に入り込んでぐっすり眠っていた　**21** was snoring いびきをかいていた

p. 34　**1** steam shovel 掘削用のパワーショベル

第4章

My Father Finds the River (エルマー　川をみつける)

p. 37　**4** just beyond a narrow strip of beach せまい海岸のすぐむこう側　**5** thick うっそうとした　**5** damp じめじめした　**7** wahoo bush ワフーの木の茂み (北米産ニシキギ属の低木)

p. 38　**2** clump 茂み　**15** muttering to itself ブツブツ言いながら

p. 39　**8** sneeze くしゃみをする

p. 42　**5** wild boars イノシシ　**6** in low solemn whispers 静かな低い声で　**8** boulders 大きな岩　**10** recent invasion 最近忍び込んだ者　**11** peels 皮　**14** upon further investigation さらに調べてみると

p. 43　**5** we're taking all this too seriously ちょっとむきになりすぎている　**7** unreliable あてにならない　**10** "Shall we retire?"「そろそろ寝るとしようか」　**10** whereupon そういって　**11** trundled back into the jungle ころがるようにジャングルのなかへもどっていった

第 5 章

My Father Meets Some Tigers（エルマー　とらにあう）

p. 45　**6** gloomy and dense 暗くてきみがわるい　**7** what room there was between them 少しでもあるすき間　**9** ferns シダ　**9** sticky ねとねとした　**17** swampy 沼のような

p. 46　**2** got stuck in the oozy, mucky mud どろどろした汚い泥にはまって動けなくなった　**3** tugged and tugged いっしょうけんめい足を引き抜こうとした　**5** wade (ぬかるみのなかを) 歩く　**16** caught at ... ...にくっついた　**17** kept tripping over ... 何回も...につまずいた　**18** were clumped so closely together that ... あまりにもぎしぎしくっついて生い茂っているので...

p. 47　**2** the deeper into the jungle he went the surer he was that ... ジャングルの奥へ行けば行くほど、...に違いないと思った　**11** clearing 空き地

p. 49　**2** were trespassing in ... ...に不法侵入している

p. 50　**2** had too much sense to say so とてもそんなことは言えないとわかっていた　**3** contradict 否定する　**7** tender 柔らかい

p. 51　**11** growled うなった

p. 54　**1** Why, you don't say! そりゃ、本当かい！　**7** Nope だめだめ

第 6 章

My Father Meets a Rhinoceros（エルマー　さいにあう）

p. 55　**5** trail みち　**9** kept a sharp lookout 警戒をおこたらなかった

p. 56　**4** afoot 進行中で　**4** intend to ... ...するつもりだ

p. 57　**8** get a head start on him 彼よりも先に出発する　**11** suspicious あやしく思う　**12** brook 小川　**16** was stooping

	down かがんでいた　　**17** by the seat of the pants ズボンのしりのところを
p. 59	**17** tusk つの　　**17** squirmed every which way あちこち体をひねった
p. 61	**4** a dab of ……をひと塗り　　**16** hoof steps 足音
p. 63	**7** sniffed 鼻をならした　　**7** trotted down 走っていった

第7章

My Father Meets a Lion（エルマー　ライオンにあう）

p. 65	**9** Ding blast it! まったくなんてこった！　　**9** go blackberrying くろいちごをとりにいく　　**13** was prancing about clawing at his mane 跳ねまわってたてがみをひっかいていた　　**14** was all snarled and full of blackberry twigs くしゃくしゃにからみあって、くろいちごの小えだがいっぱいついていた
p. 66	**13** skidded to a stop 横すべりして止まった
p. 68	**14** allowance こづかい　　**20** tidy きちんとした
p. 69	**8** forelock まえがみ　　**13** braid あむ
p. 71	**1** began busily grooming his mane たてがみをいっしょうけんめいとかし始めた

第8章

My Father Meets a Gorilla（エルマー　ゴリラにあう）

p. 73	**5** banyan tree バンヤンの木　　**15** to beat the band ものすごい勢いで
p. 74	**4** Horsefeathers! そんなばかな！　　**6** I'm going to get to the bottom of this if it's the last thing I do! 今度こそ原因をつきとめてやるぞ！

p. 75	3 Dragon Ferry りゅうの渡し場　　5 ducked behind ... ···のかげにかくれた　　6 lioness めすのライオン　　6 paraded past しゃなりしゃなりと歩いて
p. 76	2 was much too occupied looking ... her own nose あんまり気取って歩いていたので自分の鼻先しか見えなかった
p. 78	13 let go 放した　　15 "Blast those fleas!"「いまいましいノミのやつ！」　　15 raged 怒った　　21 tumbled out 飛び出した
p. 82	1 miraculous すばらしい　　4 frantically 夢中になって

第9章

My Father Makes a Bridge（エルマー　はしをかける）

p. 83	6 flagpole はたざお　　8 loop 輪　　10 crank ハンドル　　11 TO SUMMON DRAGON, YANK THE CRANK りゅうをよぶのにはハンドルをまわす　　13 REPORT DISORDERLY CONDUCT TO GORILLA りゅうがあばれたら　ゴリラに報告すること
p. 84	8 (would) choke to death 首をしめられて死ぬ　　17 hand over hand つなにぶら下がって
p. 85	4 dusk 夕暮れ　　7 have such a craving for something sweet 何か甘いものが食べたくてしかたない
p. 88	4 mighty delicious！すごくうまい！

第10章

My Father Finds the Dragon（エルマー　りゅうをみつける）

p. 90	11 seething かんかんに怒った　　12 ranting わめき散らす　　13 screeching きいきい鳴きさけぶ　　14 irate 怒った　　14 It's a trick! だまされた！
p. 91	1 stampeded down to .... ···にどどどっと押し寄せた

p. 92　**13** Just stand still. じっとしているんだよ。　**14** began to saw through the big rope 太いつなをぎしぎしと切りはじめた

p. 94　**19** sucking なめながら

p. 95　**9** laughed themselves weak お腹がいたくなるほど笑った　**13** raced around in circles ぐるぐる走り回った　 tried to turn a somersault 宙返りした

p. 98　**3** soared 飛び立った　**5** bellowing at them 大声でわめいている　**7** grinning wide grins にやにやしている　**9** feast ごちそう　**13** Bum cack! Bum cack! = Come back! Come back!!

(後注執筆：滝口峯子)

エルマーのぼうけん
My Father's Dragon

2000年 2月10日　　第 1 刷発行
2025年 4月10日　　第23刷発行

著　者　　ルース・スタイルス・ガネット
絵　　　　ルース・クリスマン・ガネット

発行者　　清田則子
発行所　　株式会社講談社　　**KODANSHA**
　　　　　〒112-8001　東京都文京区音羽2-12-21
　　　　　販売　東京03-5395-5817
　　　　　業務　東京03-5395-3615
編　集　　株式会社講談社エディトリアル
　　　　　代表　堺　公江
　　　　　〒112-0012　東京都文京区音羽1-17-18　護国寺SIAビル
　　　　　編集部　東京03-5319-2171

本文印刷　　株式会社KPSプロダクツ
カバー印刷　株式会社DNP出版プロダクツ
製　本　　　株式会社国宝社

落丁本・乱丁本は購入書店名を明記のうえ、講談社業務宛にお送りください。送料小社負担にてお取り替えいたします。なお、この本についてのお問い合わせは、講談社エディトリアル宛にお願いいたします。本書のコピー、スキャン、デジタル化等の無断複製は著作権法上での例外を除き禁じられています。本書を代行業者等の第三者に依頼してスキャンやデジタル化することはたとえ個人や家庭内の利用でも著作権法違反です。

定価はカバーに表示してあります。

© ルース・スタイルス・ガネット、ルース・クリスマン・ガネット 1948
Printed in Japan
ISBN 978-4-7700-2636-1